HEAVEN TRANSPORTS ME TO TRUE PE

APPRECIATION OF WHAT THE WORLD REALLY IS.

BEING PART OF HEAVEN REPRESENTS MY

FREEDOM.

ONLY YOU ARE CAPABLE OF FOLLOWING YOUR

DREAMS IN ORDER TO ACHIEVE WHAT YOUR

HEART AND MIND SAY, THE SKY IS NOT THE LIMIT,

THE LIMITS ARE SET BY YOU.

¡¡¡¡¡¡MACH PLANE....!!!!!

IF YOU CAN IMAGINE IT, YOU CAN DO IT

THE ONLY ONE WHO CAN LIMIT YOU IS YOU

MY NAME IS
CAPTAIN ....

LOOK THE COCKPIT

BELIEVE IN YOURSELF

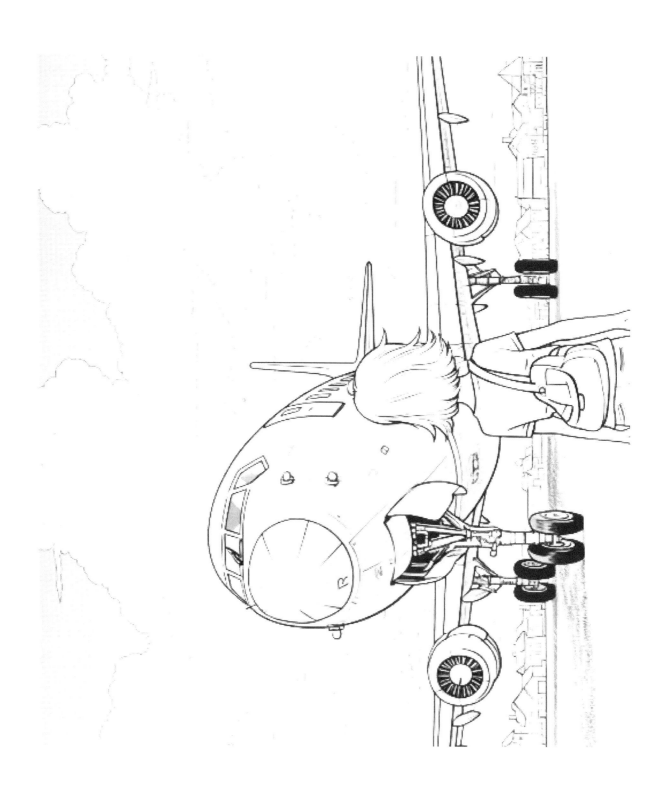

THE SKY IS NOT THE LIMIT, YOU SET THE LIMITS

LET NO ONE STOP YOU FROM ACHIEVING YOUR DREAMS

Made in the USA
Coppell, TX
27 October 2024

39227622R00017